REPORTING
FOR DUTY

Charleston, SC
www.PalmettoPublishing.com

Reporting For Duty
Copyright © 2023 by Jody L Franklin

Hardcover ISBN: 979-8-88590-443-8
Paperback ISBN: 979-8-88590-444-5
eBook ISBN: 979-8-88590-445-2

JODY FRANKLIN

REPORTING FOR DUTY

A Son's Revenge

On a beautiful summer day, Malcolm Freeman, the owner of Everyday Construction Company, and his son, Toby, are returning home after playing one-on-one basketball. The route they are traveling is a long, quiet, scenic route both enjoy because the countryside is so tranquil, and they enjoy looking at the cow pastures and horses. While driving, Malcolm begins to joke with Toby about how poorly he played against Toby and how Toby would have been as good as beaten in the game if he were in better shape. In a humorous manner, Toby asks, "Dad, do you think your age has anything to do with you losing to me?"

Sarcastically, Malcolm replies, "Toby, age is nothing but a number, and nothing gets old, young man, but clothes. And I will have you know that I was very skilled on the court back in the day."

Toby looks at his dad, rolls his eyes, and says, "Wait, let me guess, Dad. You were an all-American in your time, huh?" While still driving, with his left hand on the steering wheel, Malcolm holds up his right hand to Toby's face and tells him that he is looking at a massive hand that has much power and a threatening grip.

"Once the ball was in my hands," Malcolm says, "no opponent could take the ball until it rolled off my fingertips and landed in the basket. Jump shots and three-point shots all day. And the girls could not get enough of your dad's athleticism either."

Toby turns and looks at his dad and says, "Girls? Does Mom know about these girls?" Malcolm looks at Toby with the biggest grin on his face.

"Was your mom aware of the girls? Son, your mom was one of my main admirers. Just as your mom admired me, I admired her too," he says with a twinkle in his eye, "and our mutual admiration blessed us with an incredibly awesome son, who is almost as good as his old man on the court."

Toby chuckles at his dad's humor and lack of skills on the court. Then Toby asks his father, in a moment of sincerity and curiosity, whether he always knew he would be a successful businessman and father.

As Malcolm begins to respond, Toby interrupts and asks him if they could stop for a couple of smoothies. "Sure, why not? I would love nothing more than to reward my son with a smoothie after a game of basketball. I lost, so it only makes sense that I treat the winner and pay up." While conversating and enjoying their father-son time over a couple of strawberry smoothies, Malcolm and Toby catch a glimpse of a commercial airing that features Mayor Brown. Malcolm shares with Toby the level of appreciation and admiration he has for the mayor. Malcolm goes on to tell Toby that he and Mayor Brown went to grade school together and developed an even closer relationship when he started the business. "Throughout the years, Mayor Brown and I attended several city meetings regarding permits, regulations, and he also hired my company to build his and his wife's first home." With a proud look on his face, Malcolm tells Toby that he wants to take him by the mayor's house one day for a tour, because the mayor's house was one of the first homes built through his company. "Our building contracts have been more commercial than residential, so I am proud of the work we put into his home. Throughout the years we have stayed in touch, and Mayor Brown is one of the very few individuals I would ever go to if in need. One thing I learned through the years is that everyone needs a shoulder to lean on, a listening ear, and wise counsel from time to time. Anyway, what was it that you asked me earlier?"

"What do you mean, what did I ask you earlier," says Toby.

"Yes, son, you mentioned something about my life or my future before I got off track talking about Mayor Brown."

"Oh yes, I did!" Toby says. "Did you think you would be as successful as you are today?"

Malcolm replies, "No, Toby, I did not. But eventually I found my way, and the same goes for you. If you go to school, work hard, and apply yourself, you can have your own business as well. You can take care of your family and enjoy some of the finer things in life, Toby. A life you worked hard to earn; no handouts given to you. But you must always remember and never forget that you cannot achieve success alone. It takes a team of people who believe in you and your dream, such as your mother and Grandma Tessie. If it were not for those two women believing in me, it would have taken longer for me to achieve my goal."

"What do you mean by that, Dad?" asks Toby.

"What I mean is that your mother had to be loving, understanding, and patient with me because I worked long, rigorous hours for the business to be as successful as it is today. We had to work as a team. Most women would have felt ignored, isolated, and forgotten about, but your mother did not, because we saw the end from the beginning. And there were times your mom and I needed your Grandma Tessie to care for you when our schedules did not permit because your mother worked also at that time. My mother prepared dinner and provided much love and support throughout our journey, and thank God, we made it.

"So no, Toby, I never envisioned the business doing as well as it has, let alone being married to a beautiful woman and having a family as soon as I did. Never say never, so I will say it was not in my sights to achieve at that time due to other ideas and priorities I had for myself. However, I could not be more overjoyed about the blessings we enjoy today, which we would not have if it were not for a little inspiration from Grandma Tessie and her iron fist," Malcolm says jokingly. "As a youngster, I knew I would graduate high school, maintain a mediocre job, and hang out with friends. You know, doing things you and your peers enjoy doing. Eventually, I would have desired a wife and family, but first I wanted to enjoy my youth, because I always felt as though I was robbed of my teenage years due to the loss of my father early on. As a result of your grandfather's sudden death, my direction in life and desire to care and take things seriously had changed. I did not approach life as I should have. However, I graduated from high school for several reasons, and one of those reasons was your grandmother. Your Grandma Tessie always wanted the best for her four children, and with me being the oldest, she was harder on me. I had to help Momma take care of all my siblings. So, as you can see, having a family and career was not in my line of priorities at the time, because I already had that, and not necessarily by choice. That is why I was rusty today on the basketball court—because I had to drop out of basketball practice to hurry home to help care for my siblings until Momma made it home.

"Boy," Malcolm says to Toby. "Your daddy wanted to play and enjoy life with his friends, because that is what a teenager is supposed to do, so I thought."

Toby asks his father, "Dad, are you mad at Grandma Tessie for not letting you be a kid?"

Malcolm replies, "In the beginning I experienced so many different emotions—anger, sadness, loneliness, bitterness, and confusion—because I did not know better. I did not want to accept my dad being gone forever. How could I fill the shoes of such a great father and husband?

"Those were my thoughts, then, and the challenges I faced and allowed to consume me as a teenager. It took time, but I had to learn that my mom really needed me, as much as I needed her, which I would soon find out. Your grandmother did not ask to be a widow. She did not ask to lose her husband. So, to answer your question, my anger turned into appreciation for my mother and respect for her love and strength to continue after my dad passed away. Your Grandma Tessie did what she had to do to keep a roof over our heads, food on the table, and a safe place for her children to be raised, and if that called for assuming more responsibility as the oldest, then so be it. I know my mom loved us. She was our father and mother at that time. My mother gave us the best gifts that life can give, which were, love, wisdom, and a solid foundation."

"Wisdom?" Toby repeats in an intrigued state.

"Yes, Grandma shared her wisdom with us, which taught us how to be leaders and not followers. She taught us to always have respect for ourselves, elders, and others," Malcolm says. "She told us to try to always walk in love with your brothers and sisters. Not just your biological siblings, but also your sisters and brothers in Christ."

"I hear you, Dad, but some people abuse your kindness, mistaking it for weakness. Some folks will test your levels, but I hear what you are saying."

Malcolm says, "No, Toby, do not hear what I am saying; receive what I am saying. Try to understand and apply what I am explaining to your life. Your Grandma Tessie always said, 'You get more with honey than you do with vinegar.'"

"Huh? What does that mean?" Toby questions.

"It means if you treat people with love and kindness, despite their attitude and ways toward you, you can never lose by showing love, mercy, and understanding. You can never go wrong being the bigger person and taking your cares to the Lord. If we want mercy, we must show mercy to others."

"OK, OK, Dad, I get it! Be the bigger person and walk away."

"That is why I can sit here today proudly as your father and say I am successful. Not just as a business owner, father, and husband, but also as a son, because I stopped and listened to Momma when she talked. I absorbed all her teachings like a sponge and applied them to my life. As I got older, I did not know the same advice she gave me would be the advice I would share with my child one day, and that child happens to be you," Malcolm says with a wink. "Grandma Tessie's teachings kept me out of trouble down the road. You do not have to be educated, as far as school is concerned, to be taught by the best and to get through life. After all, your grandmother was not educated at the time. She had only completed the eighth grade when she met my father and married, but Momma was a wise woman, beyond her years. You cannot buy wisdom, son; either you have it or you do not. You know, just like me, your dad. You see my debonair looks, style, and grace. Either you got it, or you do not," Malcolm says as he laughs and slaps his thigh. "The wisdom your granny imparted in her children is priceless. One day, Toby, you may encounter an Educated Fool in this world, "Educated Fool". Yes, a person with a ton of book smarts and degrees but does not have an ounce of common sense. All they know is what they read and have been taught from a book."

"Now that is a scary thought," Toby says with a look of disappointment and disbelief. "Dad, you talk a lot about Grandma, but why do you speak so little about Granddaddy Otis?"

After a moment of silence, Malcolm tells Toby with tears in his eyes that it is getting late, and they have been in the smoothie parlor for over an hour. "Your mother is going to become worried about us, so let us go. We can discuss further in the car. Is that, OK?" Malcom asks Toby.

Once in the car, Toby asks his dad to please share a story about his father. "All right, my dad was a willful, hardworking man who believed in loyalty, trust, taking care of your responsibilities, and being accountable for your own actions. He was no stranger to arduous work. A man who did not know when to stop, pause, and take in all that life had to offer. He believed taking time for hobbies, relaxation, or any sort of leisure was time wasted. There was always work to be done, in his eyes, and money to be made, so time was of the essence. My dad would always say, 'Idle time can be the devil's playhouse.'"

"What did he mean by that?" Toby asks.

"Too much time on your hands can cause a person to venture into unproductive mischief. Finding yourself involved in things that could land you in trouble or jail. That is why my father stayed busy and made us children stay busy. We had to earn our keep around the house. There was no such thing as downtime or playtime to him because he felt there were important things to be done. He would always say, 'Every creature God created knows their role and responsibility to survive without instruction. It is just innate. So why is man the only creation that needs instructions, bribes, or coercion to meet a need or responsibility that is required for them and their family to survive?' If you must tell or ask a person to meet an obvious need that is very much necessary, Granddaddy Otis would call that person lazy and trifling. Your Granddaddy Otis worked from sunup to sundown. We were in bed when he came home at night, and he was off to work before we got up the next morning. Therefore, our time with dad was on the weekends. He was a prideful man who did not care much for handouts. Sadly enough, the same standards he lived by were the standards by which he died. We knew our dad loved us, because he worked hard to take care of Mom, us, and the home he built for his family. However, the stubborn side of him could not comprehend when enough was enough. Your grandfather never went to the doctor, never knew what relaxation, meditation, or peace was, I do not think. He worked so much I do not think he ever grasped and embraced the full essence of family and togetherness. He had a mass or knot growing on his hand that he never addressed and would tell your Grandma Tessie he hit his hand working and it was nothing to worry about, so he thought. Your grandfather was diagnosed with epithelioid sarcoma, which is a rare, slow-growing type of soft-tissue cancer, at the young age of thirty-five. In my heart, I think dad thought if he ignored the mass and wrapped it up, then it would heal itself and would take the worry from his wife. So, what made Grandaddy Otis go to the doctor? Toby, he only went because while the mass did not necessarily get any bigger, it began causing him intense pain in his hands and joints, and, you know, he needed his hands to work. By the time my mom and dad found out what the mass was, it was too late. As much as his death hurt and devastated me, I am so grateful the good Lord allowed him not to suffer. It seemed that just as soon as he received the diagnosis, he was gone, just like that," Malcolm says with tears in his eyes and a trembling voice. "I believe my dad would have lived a longer life had he only taken a break to care for himself, listened to Momma Tessie, followed doctor's orders, and rested. Then maybe his life could have been extended and he could have had more time with the family, making memories, but as he would always say, rest is for the dead. I honestly believe that just as much as my mother was worried and afraid, your grandfather was too. He wanted to maintain his rugged and tough exterior and acknowledging his illness and not being able to work as much as was needed, according to his standards, was a sign of weakness, because his family and friends would have to step in to provide for us. Anyhow, he transitioned nine months after the diagnosis. He was only thirty-five, one month shy of his thirty-sixth birthday. Seeing all the hurt and devastation my mother went through after the loss of her husband—that experience made me mature fast. However, I was still in high school, young, and making foolish decisions from time to time. From my point of view, it did not seem hard for me to step up and help Mom, because I had my dad to model after. Who was a perfect example of a leader and protector from my perspective? Did I want to sacrifice my time to help care for my siblings instead of going to school dances and out on dates? No, but I had no choice; my mom depended on me. If there was anything to be learned from my father, I learned how to assume responsibility, not be selfish, and understand that for every action there is a reaction and consequence. I also learned to be confident in who I am and to pause, stop, and enjoy each moment God gives. It is imperative you grasp and understand the concept of working to live and not living to work. To take time for your loved ones. That is why you and me spending time together is so precious and very much enjoyable to me. You and your mom mean the world to me. If I had to do it all over again, I would, just to become the man I am today. Toby, I believe with God's grace and Grandma Tessie's guidance, I evolved into an all-right young man," Malcolm says with a smile on his face. "Quality time is so important in a family. You do not know how much I would give just to sit on my dad's lap one more time and have him hug me and turn to me with those thick eyebrows and stern grin. Just to hear him say, 'You are a mighty fine boy.' I do not fault my dad for doing what he knew to do. I cannot be mad. Your Granddaddy Otis was the best man, father, and husband he knew how to be. We could not have asked for anything more in a dad, Malcolm says. "You know what the eerie part about my dad's death is?"

Toby replies, "What's that, Dad?"

"I was around your age when my dad passed away in his sleep one night. He just stopped breathing. I remember us kids waking up to Mom screaming at the top of her lungs. I mean, Toby, Momma cried so hard I thought she was going to wake the neighborhood. Never take life for granted. When we were little, we would stay up waiting on your granddaddy to come home, because we never got to see him in the mornings before school and in the evenings before bedtime. He was always working, and Mom would feed us and put us to bed before he ever made it home. One night we wanted to be a little mischievous and go against Momma. We stayed up as late as we could, waiting to say good night to Dad, and Momma caught us up waiting, but she did not say a word, so we thought she was OK with us being up so late. Not! Your grandma came in that room with that switch, and before we knew it, we were asleep or sleepwalking, because I saw cows jumping over the moon. If we were not asleep, that switch sure helped put us in a sleep state. My goodness, Toby, that was a moment to remember. From that day forth, Momma never had to worry about us going to sleep. I believe I beat everyone to sleep after that night."

"Why did grandma spank y'all for wanting to see your dad?"

"She got onto us because we disobeyed what she asked us to do, and each morning we would moan, groan, and cry about getting up, saying we were sleepy and tired. She had four children to wash up, feed, and get ready for school each day. She said, 'I will have your dad come in before he dozes off to sleep.' That is what she told us. We were sad, but we understood after she let that switch do the talking. Reluctantly, we all said, 'Yes ma'am.' Dad would come in each night, kiss, and see about us before going to bed, and occasionally he would leave a nickel on the dresser for each of us. The nickel signified his love and confirmed his presence. Dad must have been tired that night and, I guess, in so much pain, because Momma found him the next morning curled in a fetal position, not breathing, still fully clothed and with droplets of blood running from his mouth. Dad knew he would transition and leave us for good that night, and he did not want to alert Momma, which explains him dying on the couch and not in the bed. Daddy never missed a day or night sleeping with his 'B. G. Tessie.' That is what Daddy would call your grandmother; he called her Beautiful Girl Tessie. Come to think of it, that is why he left us a quarter instead of a nickel the night of his death. Dad never gave us more than a nickel when he came home, and we were already asleep. That was his way of showing us his love. The quarter represented his love. He loved us more than we could ever know or expect, so always expect the unexpected. We woke up expecting to possibly see a nickel, but instead we saw a big ole quarter. My dad leaving all of us with a quarter was more than we could have ever imagined."

"So, what happened to your quarter, Dad?"

"Believe it or not, Toby, I still have that same quarter and vowed to never spend or lose it. I will show you my secret place when we return home. Toby, I am not speaking ill or against my father's way of doing things, or saying I am a better man, but what I will say is that when you know better, you should always do better. However, I will say that he taught me how to embrace every moment the Lord gives to me and to never stress about and consume myself with things I cannot change or have control over. As your grandmother helped me, I helped and encouraged her also. Shortly after my father passed, your grandmother set the example by taking night classes and eventually furthering her education. She and I were in school together. I went to school in the day and she at night, so she could still be of assistance to me, and your mom as needed. Through perseverance and determination, your grandmother received her PhD in family counseling, and that is how she began working with hurting women and in family counseling. Another important lesson your mother and I learned was to never put anything before family. The structure for our household is God, family, work, and church. Your personal life should never interfere with your professional life, or vice versa. The recipe for success is when one learns how to manage and prioritize family and work. I am going to share a story with you, a story I have not shared since that day. Always remember, one unwise decision and operating in disobedience can cost you your life. As I told you earlier, when Dad died, I had so many responsibilities that I felt like I was drowning in expectations. Whenever I had an opportunity to hang out with my friends, I did. There were times when I deliberately stayed out past curfew because I never knew when the next time would be. It was Friday, February 16, 1990, a day I will never forget. It was me, Gerald, Paul, and Cedric hanging out in front of old man Simon's store. Back then, the corner store was the hangout spot for teens, and even though Mr. Simon never favored children hanging around his establishment, he never ran me and my friends off as he did others. I believe it was partly because we showed respect and never brought trouble to his store. We never wanted to make business bad for him, so we would hang out by the side of the store, several feet away. Anyway, Cedric and Paul said they needed to use the bathroom and were going into old man Simon's store, which confused us, because Mr. Simon had a porta potty out back. The restroom inside was for him and his employees only. Anyway, we did not question them and waited outside as they walked in. Unbeknownst to us, Cedric and Paul had plotted to steal candy and drinks while Mr. Simon was cleaning the shelves, his back turned. Gerald and I, still ignorant and oblivious to the ordeal inside the store, were laughing and talking with a couple of female classmates when we witnessed Cedric and Paul running out of the store and down the street. While standing in complete and total shock, still unclear on what had taken place, me, Gerald, and the girls saw old man Simon run out of the store with a gun in hand, chasing both boys, aiming, and firing a shot into Cedric's back. Everything happened so fast, in the blink of an eye. All I remember is Cedric falling to his knees, dropping face-first onto the pavement, and dying instantly. Gerald and I were scared straight. It felt like we had cement shoes on; we could not move. It was hard to comprehend what we had just witnessed, the murder of our good friend. Before long, Mr. Simon walked back up to the store and put the pistol in our faces and told us not to move. He said, 'The two of you wait here until the police comes.' As I looked into Mr. Simon's eyes, all I remember was a blank stare, a look I had never seen before. He looked at us as though we were strangers, a group of boys he had never known or seen. I did not see an ounce of distress, remorse, or any type of emotion on his face whatsoever. We knew Mr. Simon was grumpy, but never to the point of taking a life. All I could think about at that time was my mother, exceeding curfew, and what was she going to do to me when she heard the news? All kinds of thoughts started running through my mind. Why was I not home on time and abiding by mother's curfew? I knew that night would be the last and final night my friends would see me for a long time. Although I do not think my friends meant for things to unfold the way they did. They were just trying to have a little fun with Mr. Simon, trying to see if they could get away with something. You know how children do. Even you get into mischief sometimes. I am sure they would have never taken anything from him if they had an inkling of him taking one of their lives. There was no reason for a life to be taken, but that goes to show, you can never underestimate a person. Everyone has a breaking point, and apparently that night was old man Simon's breaking point. We were no strangers to him; the store was a common, daily spot for the youth. Gerald and I just did not understand why Mr. Simon did not let them go and notify their parents and have Cedric and Paul complete community hours to pay back their debts. The town was small, and no one was a stranger. Anyway, me, Gerald, and the girls waited for the police to arrive."

"Do you think your friends who were playing and taking the candy were right?" Toby asks.

Malcolm replies, "No, son, stealing is never OK. I do not care how you view the situation or the intentions behind stealing. Never take anything you cannot afford. If you desire something bad enough, then you should patiently wait until you save enough money to purchase it yourself. Just as Cedric lost his life that night, Mr. Simon lost merchandise that he sold to make money to support himself. However, I do think the situation could have been handled differently so no lives were lost. Sadly enough, their fun turned into the demise of a good friend. Paul was eventually convicted of robbery and sentenced to ten years for a prank gone wrong. The only reason Gerald and I did not get charged was because Karen and Linda, the two girls we were talking to that very night, told the police we did not know about their plan to rob Mr. Simon, and they were our alibis. Eventually, the girls were released to return home, while Gerald and I were interrogated a little while longer. I will never forget the two officers who questioned us and were the first to arrive on the scene. One of the officers was an older veteran, and the other was younger, approximately early thirties. A 'rookie' cop."

Toby asks Malcolm if a rookie officer is considered an inexperienced officer. "Yes, son, pretty much. I remember hearing the rookie ask his partner if he was happy that another one was down."

"Say what?"

"Yes, the younger officer made a statement regarding another Black male being killed, and Mr. Simon doing the community a favor."

"Wow!" Toby responds. "Dad, that is so sad."

"I do not think the veteran officer was aware I heard the rookie's statement or cared if I heard it, because he never corrected the rookie and without saying it, basically agreed. My friend Paul was never the same after serving ten years in prison. I stayed in contact with his mother and one of his brothers throughout the years before losing contact. After Paul's conviction, Gerald and I never shared the close connection we once had as brothers. I thought Gerald and I would become inseparable, but everyone handles loss differently. After graduating high school, Grandma Tessie moved us to Kentucky for a new and fresh start, which is another reason I lost contact with Gerald. Before I moved, I took the initiative to visit Gerald, who became a hermit and very isolated, which was understandable. Gerald had never experienced the loss of someone close to him, but I had when my father passed away. I am sure Paul had to mature faster than he could have imagined because he carried the guilt of Cedric's death with him every day. The guilt consumed him so badly that he turned to drugs for relief, but many say he was exposed to drugs while incarcerated. So, as you can see, Toby, that is why me and your mom stress the importance of accountability and making wise decisions in life and being a leader and a young man of integrity. The death of a loved one is not anything I want you to ever experience anytime soon."

"Dad is that why you never go back to visit?" asks Toby.

"Toby, I have gone back home on several occasions. You do not remember because you were a toddler the last time I visited. Would you like to go and visit my hometown?" Malcolm asks.

"Yes, sir, I would love to see your home away from home for myself."

"All right, son, it is a deal. After you graduate high school in the next few months, we will go, before you leave for college. That will give me the opportunity to show you around and for you to see what your father does professionally. After receiving my degree and contractor's license, I went back home and worked on a few development projects. No matter how established and accomplished you become in life, never forget your beginnings and where you started. It is your roots that keep you humble, grounded, and appreciative of all your achievements in life. Just as easy as success comes, success can go. So, I will give Mayor Brown a call tomorrow."

"Dad, I hope I never lose you and Mom," says Toby.

"Let us not think of the things to come. Let us just enjoy each and every moment we have together, just me, you, and Mom," replies Malcolm.

"That sounds like a deal," Toby says with a smile.

"I can tell you one thing, Toby, after witnessing the loss of Cedric and Paul going to jail, your Grandmother Tessie never had an ounce of trouble from me. Momma Tessie and my siblings got tired of seeing me every day. Man, you could not pay me to hang out or leave home. I was an upstanding citizen, straight as a board," Malcolm says with tears in his eyes from laughter.

"Wait, Dad, you did not tell me why Mr. Simon hated the children hanging around his store so much."

"Are you sure you want to major in engineering in college?" asks Malcolm.

"Yes, I am sure, why do you ask?"

"Cause you ask questions like a news reporter. All right, I will share what I can, because we are almost home, and I am ready to see your momma, and I am sure she is ready to see us. Anyway, Mr. Simon moved from Virginia, established his business in the neighborhood when I was very young. A toddler you can say, but only after Cedric's death, did I learn the history of the Simons. I heard that he was one of the nicest men you could ever meet. Their store was known as the community's favorite. The landscape of the store and customer service was superb. He only hired the best of the best employees. He and his wife were known to give back and assist the less fortunate. He had a big heart; he allowed customers on fixed incomes to get items they needed on IOUs, and the customers always paid their debts on time, so the respect between the Simons and customers was mutual. The parents in the neighborhood had much respect for them. Parents knew where to find their children, and if the children ever did anything wrong, they knew the Simons would reprimand and correct the children also. But one day Mr. Simon caught his daughter, Maggie Girl, talking to

Skip Rogers, a nice-looking young guy who all the girls in town went crazy over. Mr. Simon was very protective of his little girl, so much so that he did not want her to befriend anyone of the male persuasion. They say he was so old fashioned that his wife and daughter had to wear dresses down to their ankles with long sleeves. He always believed a woman's body is to be left to the imagination. I cannot argue with that, because certain things should be left to a man's imagination, but long sleeves in the summertime was a bit much if you ask me. Nevertheless, after a year of sneaking around, Maggie Girl and Skip ran off together, eloped, and married without her parents' approval or permission. Maggie was twenty and Skip was twenty-eight. Mr. Simon did not see his dear Maggie again until twelve months later, and by then there was a little one in her hands and no Skip Rogers to be found. I was told that everyday Maggie Girl would sit by the window crying, awaiting Skip's return. She always believed he would come back one day. Days turned into weeks, and weeks turned into months, and months turned into a couple of years of waiting, which led to Maggie's deep depression, one she never recovered from. Her depression was so severe that she could only find peace in death. Early one morning, Mr. Simon found his little girl slumped over dead behind his store while taking out the trash. Maggie bled to death from the cutting of her wrist. From what I was told, Maggie Girl was never the same once she returned home. She never knew how to forgive herself for hurting her father and mother and losing the only man she ever loved besides her father. In the pocket of her dress was a note written to her lost love, Skip, and it read, 'I left my life and dreams behind to chase yours. I thought you would always love and care for me until we were no more, but apparently me and your son were never enough for you. My heart longs and hurts for you daily, each time I look at the bundle of joy we created. I do not know what to do. My father was right; I was wrong. That is why I can no longer go on. Roses are red and violets are blue, goodbye my love, the love I once knew.' After Mr. Simon found his daughter dead, he was never the same. His wife suffered a massive heart attack because of Maggie Girl's suicide. Before long, Mr. Simon could no longer afford to care for his wife at home, once she had returned from a three-month stint in the hospital after the heart attack, so he placed her in a nursing home, where she soon expired. Now alone, saddened and still in disbelief, Mr. Simon sent his only grandchild to live with his sister in another state. He sent his sister money every month for his grandson because he could not work and provide the nurturing the boy needed. Oddly enough, Skip never came to town to find his son or to rectify what he had put Mr. Simon's daughter and the entire family through. Apparently, those events resulted in Mr. Simon becoming grumpy and distant, and never trusting a living soul again. Never have fun at another person's expense, which is why my friends are not here today. They found fun at the expense of Mr. Simon and not on their own. You do not have to steal, kill, or destroy to get ahead in life. All you must do is work for what you want," says Malcolm.

"Dad where is Mr. Simon's grandson now?" asks Toby.

"I am not quite sure, Toby, but what I have been told is that many years later, when Mr. Simon passed away, his grandson came and took over ownership of the store and kept it thriving in remembrance of his grandma, grandpa, and mother, but I am not certain. I have only returned home a handful of times and never think to go by old man Simon's store.

"That is commendable, Dad, that his grandson keeps his legacy alive by owning and managing the store. See that is what I want to do when I graduate from college. I want to own and oversee your business."

"Wait, what? You want to own my business?" Malcolm asks.

"Yeah—wait, I mean yes, sir."

Malcolm looks at Toby and tells him to pump his brakes. "How about I own my business, and you run and operate your own? Hold your horses now. No! How about I continue to own and operate my business and you start your own company and I serve as co-owner? To me son, that sounds like a sweet deal, if I say so myself.

"However, it would be nice working with my son, but never for him…ha ha ha! Generational wealth is the goal and should be the goal for anyone. And, son, always strive to be better than your old man. That is all me and your mom have ever wanted for you. To live a full, healthy life that you will be proud of. If you are going to be a proud man, then be proud of your own accomplishments in life, and never be afraid to admit when you are wrong and learn from your mistakes. When you are an entrepreneur, you can make your own hours, and that was my desire after losing Grandaddy Otis and my friend. My entire outlook on life had to change. Man, if it did not, you and I may not have been afforded the opportunities to do what we enjoy doing, which is spending lots of quality time together. One day when you get married and have children, Toby, you will learn that family comes first, because tomorrow is not promised to you. I have no regrets when it comes to the sacrifices and love I have invested in you and your mom. You and your mother are my world, and I love both of you with all my heart. Now let us go in the house to see your mom."

Months later, as promised, Toby is wakened by the loud noise of his father bursting into his room with a suitcase and a smile. "Toby, today is the day, son."

"What are you talking about, Dad?"

"Are you serious?" Malcolm asks. "What is today?"

"Today is June 13, 2004."

"That is right. You and I have a road trip to take before you leave for college, young man."

Instantly, Toby jumps out of bed, packs his clothes, and runs out of the house before turning around and giving his mother a big hug and kiss. While driving, Toby looks at Malcolm and says, "Dad, you kept your word. We are on our way to see your hometown. I cannot wait to hear some of the stories Mayor Brown has for me. Stories you have kept from me and did not want me to know."

After a two-week-long visit to Malcolm's hometown, he and Toby travel back to their hotel after enjoying a lavish dinner their final night in town. They leave the next day. While driving, Malcolm becomes a bit drowsy and swerves a little before suggesting Toby take the wheel and drive the remaining distance. At that moment, Malcolm and Toby are blinded by bright, flashing lights. Malcolm looks in the rearview mirror, and mumbles, "Are you serious? Cops!" Malcolm looks over at Toby and tells him to relax. "Everything will be OK. I swerved a little while driving, so they are probably just doing a routine stop to ensure we are OK and not under any type of influence. Everything will be just fine; I have done nothing wrong, so call your mom and let her know what is going on, because she is expecting my call. She knows it does not take more than fifteen minutes to get from the restaurant to the hotel."

Just before Toby begins dialing, one of the officers instructs them to place their hands out of the window. Toby, in a nervous state, asks Malcolm what to do. "Do I call Mom, Dad?"

"No, son, do as you are told, and place your hands out the window as the officer instructed." While patiently waiting for several minutes, unsure of the ordeal, Malcolm yells out the window, "Hello, officer, what is the problem? What is going on?" With no response, Malcolm shouts again, "Hello, officers. I have my son with me. Why am I being pulled over?" Again, in a raised voice, Malcolm yells his name and asks if he can step out of the car.

An officer responds and says, "Shut your mouth, boy, and wait until I give you further instructions. Do you understand?"

Malcolm responds with a bit of irritation but in a respectful tone. "I am with my young son. Please watch how you speak to me."

The officer responds again with, "What did you say, boy?"

Then Toby shouts, "Dad, no! Please do not say anything else!"

"OK, relax, son. I am only communicating with the officer. I have the right to speak. There is freedom of speech."

"Oh yeah, freedom for who? Not us, apparently," Toby replies.

Finally, Officer Michael S. Brite approaches the driver's side window with his gun drawn, shouting, "Put your hands where I can see them. Did you hear what I said? Put your hands where I can see them!"

Malcolm says, "Officer, my hands are where you can see them, so what is your problem?"

"Do not ask me what my problem is. What is your problem, boy? You were speeding and swerving back there."

"Officer, you are correct; I did swerve. However, I did not speed. Me and my son are on our way back to the hotel, and I am a bit sleepy, so I was pulling over so my son could drive the remaining distance."

"Do you have drugs or any concealed weapons in this car?" asks the officer.

"I beg your pardon, drugs? Just who do you think we are?" Malcolm asks. "I just told you that my son and I were heading back to the hotel when you pulled us over. We have a long drive home tomorrow, so I would appreciate you writing the ticket if that is what you choose to do or let us go. I have broken no laws."

The officer requests a license and registration. "That is right, nice and slow. I would not want there to be a casualty, now, would you?" Officer Brite asks.

"Did you just threaten me in front of my son, officer?" Malcolm responds.

"You know what? You ask too many questions," says the officer. "I guess you think you are something, driving around town in your BMW M5." As the officer looks at Malcolm's license, he says, "Well now, Malcolm Freeman, just what is it that you do for a living, sir? I am familiar with your kind."

"Excuse me, officer," Malcolm replies. "My kind? And just what is my kind?"

The officer shines the bright light in Malcolm's face, laughs, and says, "Just what I am looking at."

"Wow," Malcolm responds. "Toby, do you remember what Dad taught you?"

"What are you talking about, Dad?"

"You shut your mouth, boy; I ask the questions around here, not you."

Speaking defiantly, Malcolm says. "Give respect when respect is due, and always know who you are." After several minutes of consistent harassment and belittling, irritated and feeling very much disrespected, Malcolm looks into the officer's eyes and says, "well let me see". I work an honest job, making more money in a month than you make in six, you are arrogant, self-righteous, spineless coward of an officer. You give honest officers with integrity a bad name." As Malcolm proceeds to look forward, with his hands still on the steering wheel, he tells the officer, "If you want to know what I do for a living, you figure it out. One thing I know for sure, is that I have done more for this city than you and your partner." And it was at that very moment that the officer proceeds to open Malcolm's door, drag him out, and start beating him while Toby looked on. In a panicked state, Toby grabs the phone and attempts to call his mother while yelling at the officer, telling him to leave his father alone, but he cannot get a signal. Toby attempts to call his mother again, but to no avail. Then Officer John B. Landen, the other officer, walks up to Toby's passenger-side door, reaches in, and grabs Toby's hand with so much pressure that Toby drops the phone and is unsuccessful in calling his mother.

"Who do you think you're calling, son?" asks Landen. "You must not know where you are. Out in these parts, there is no connection, so please try again and again to call whoever you like boy, the call will not go through, you little nigger. You see, there is no reception out here," Landen says in a sarcastic manner. He continues taunting Toby. "Come on now, make that call, boy. Oh, let me guess, you want to call your mommy, huh? Is that who you want to call? Or better yet, why don't you try calling ghostbusters?" Landen says with laughter. "I suggest, boy, you stay calm before you get a good lashing like your pappy over there on that ground. Listen, it sounds like my partner is giving your daddy a good working out. A punishment he is long overdue for, just like you, monkey." Then suddenly, Toby forcefully pushes the car door open, knocking Landen to the ground, and runs toward Officer Brite, hoping to help his father.

As he proceeds to charge at Officer Brite, he hears the gun click. "Stop right there, boy, before I blow you away," says Landen, and from behind Landen begins wrestling and choking Toby to the point of Toby passing out, but before Toby succumbs to the choke hold, he witnesses his father being severely and relentlessly beaten and insulted by the other officer with a nightstick.

Suddenly, Toby regains consciousness, and in a frantic state, Toby yells out, "Dad, are you OK?"

With the little-to-no strength Malcolm has remaining, he says, "Yes, son, please stay calm and do what the officers say." He covers his head to the best of his ability, trying to cushion the blows. Before leaving, Brite lands one more fatal blow to

Malcolm's head. He kicks Malcolm so hard you can hear the bones in his neck snap. The officers speed away before travelers come down the road. As Malcolm lies motionless, bleeding from his head and mouth, Toby holds his father's lifeless body in his arms and talks softly in his father's ear, telling him how much he loves him and that he will be OK.

"God got you, Dad, so no worries," Toby repeats as he musters the strength to remain calm and strong for his father. Toby belts out a scream and says, "Dear Lord, please have mercy and send someone to help my dad." A couple of minutes later, an older couple traveling along the road from a night out on the town sees Toby and his father on the side of the road. David and Sara Willhurst stop their car after discovering Toby lying over his father's lifeless body, crying. Suddenly, David jumps out of the car and tells Sara to stay there as he approaches the bloody, unidentifiable body to see what assistance he can provide to the beaten gentleman and his son. David calls the police, requesting an ambulance immediately to their location.

Meanwhile, David calls Sara out of the car, asking her to console Toby as he continues to aid and talk to Malcolm, trying to keep him awake. David shakes Malcolm and says to Toby, "Son, what is his name?"

Toby replies, "Malcolm, sir."

"Malcolm, Malcolm," David repeats. "Sir, can you hear me? We have help on the way, so hang in there."

Malcolm does not reply, but then Malcolm awakens for a moment and says, "Two cops."

"What? What did you say?" David, confused and puzzled, asks Malcolm in desperation to please stay awake, but Malcolm goes into an unconscious state. David Willhurst turns to Toby and asks, "Son, who assaulted your dad? What did they look like? What were their names, and what were they wearing?" At that moment the emergency medical team and police arrive, making David's efforts to gather any additional information more difficult.

Toby says to David, "I don't know, I just don't know, sir" as tears roll down his face. Mrs. Willhurst pulls Toby closer to her for comfort and to ensure he knows he will be OK, and he is with good people.

Shortly after Malcolm arrives at the hospital, badly wounded, he is rushed into emergency surgery. Still in the ICU six months later, Malcolm never regains consciousness and succumbs to his injuries. Malcolm's autopsy report reveals that he had suffered internal bleeding, a fractured skull and spine, and a severed spleen caused by blunt force trauma.

Toby can never get past that tragic day, but he knows he and his mother have to carry on with life. "There is no other way I can be my father molded me and raised me to be the man I am today, and I am a go-getter." The untimely death of his father postpones his dreams and school for a few years. Toby, now twenty-one years of age, tells his mother that he wants to attend the police academy.

Toby's mother, speechless and confused, says, "What did you just say, Toby?"

"Yes, ma'am, you heard me, Ma. I want to become a police officer."

"Toby, I just thought maybe you would want to pursue your engineering degree since your father's passing. You have been helping me with your father's business, so what changed?"

"I know and understand you are not pleased or in agreement with my decision, but this is my life, and I must live it as I see fit. You never have to worry, Ma. You and Dad raised me right. I am a God-fearing young man with integrity and purpose, and I feel my purpose currently is in law enforcement."

"Toby, I hear what you are saying. However, I do not understand why, son, after you saw what your father went through and the devastation it caused our family." With a twinkle in his eye and a heart of sweet revenge, Toby tells his mother not to worry but to know that for every action there is a reaction and consequence. "What...Toby, what in the world does that mean?" his mother asks. "Toby, you saw what happened to your father. So why would you want to work with some low-down, cowardly police officers who are only tough behind the badge? Grant you me, I know all officers are not that way, but it is so hard to trust, son. What if someone else experienced an awful officer and takes it out on you because they see you all the same? Which is not fair and is not true."

"Ma do not worry. I will cross that bridge when I get to it. By the way, I will be moving out and moving back to Dad's hometown."

"You are doing what, young man?" Toby's mother shouts. "OK, first you stab me in the heart with your career choice, and now you are telling me that you are going to work in the same city as the officers that murdered your father?"

"Yes, ma'am," says Toby.

"Well, stick a fork in me and call me done. Not only do you stick a knife in my heart, but you twist the knife to do more damage?"

"Calm down, it is going to be OK. Really, it is," Toby says to his mother as he hugs and embraces her. "I do not expect you to like my decision. However, I would love and appreciate your support. Sometimes, Ma, we must agree to disagree, and this is one of those times."

Toby moves to his father's hometown and enrolls in the police academy under his abbreviated last name, so no one will suspect who he is. After six long months of training, Toby graduates from the police academy and becomes an officer of the law. Toby's captain tells him that he is assigning him to one of the precinct's finest officers. An officer with a lot of street knowledge, respect, and skills. The captain goes on to tell Toby that

Brite is very well known and is held in high regard in the town. "Officer Brite has been with the force for thirty-five years."

"Wow, thirty-five years," Toby repeats.

"Yes, sir," says the captain. "If you are going to train and learn the ropes, I want you to learn from the best, OK, rookie?" So, Captain Johns instructs Chief Bell to assign Toby to Patrol Duty with Officer Michael S. Brite, one of the precinct's veteran officers with a lot of insight and knowledge of the streets. After a year and a half of partnership, Toby, at the rightful age of twenty-five, has gained a great deal of his partner's trust. While on duty, Toby's partner stops a car that did not make a complete stop at the traffic light before turning. Then suddenly the partner hits the lights on the patrol car and shouts, "Son of a Bitch"

Toby, startled, looks at him and asks, "What is the problem?"

"That pillock did not make a complete stop at the traffic light before turning, that is the problem." After a short pursuit, the driver pulls over. With the lights from the patrol car shining bright on the driver's car, Toby and his partner continue sitting in the patrol car. Unsure of his partner's hesitation and delay, Toby proceeds to get out of the car to speak to the driver, when he is forcefully grabbed by his partner and asked, "What are you doing?"

Toby immediately responds, "I am going to speak to the driver."

"Do not get out of this patrol car."

With a bothered and confused look, Toby asks, "What did you say?"

"You heard me. Do not get out of this car." With a smirk on his face, the partner says, "The best form of intimidation is making the driver wait and sweat. Let them wait like a sitting duck or a piece of pork fat in the sun. Who cares, responds Brite? I do not, and neither should you." Instantly, Toby has a flashback of his father's encounter with an officer, a very similar scenario. It feels as though the hair on Toby's neck has begun to stand up. Besides Toby, who knows where they are heading? Us stopping them could have prevented a drug deal or them picking up a prostitute. It is at that very moment that Toby gets out of the car to speak with the driver of the vehicle they pulled over. Not one time does Toby's partner get up to render any type of assistance to him, like checking the passenger side or the back seat of the driver's vehicle. He just lets Toby address the matter himself. Eventually, Toby releases the driver with a warning. The remainder of the evening is cold and tense, with neither officer speaking a word to each other.

Subsequently, Toby cannot rest and has many sleepless nights as a result of his partner's treatment of the driver. Toby cannot dismiss the similarities of that traffic stop to the traffic stop he and his father encountered that fatal night, and unfortunately, Toby cannot identify either officer due to the blinding lights and their badges not being visible. As time goes on, the trust between the partners continues to grow, and Toby is exposed to more and more unlawful and unethical practices by his partner and other members of the police force. The more exposure Toby experiences, the more his spiritual torment grows. Even though Toby never takes part in lawless acts, he feels guilty because he was present and did nothing to help the victims. The only way he can combat the emotional, psychological, and spiritual warfare inside is through prayer and reciting Deuteronomy 32:35 daily: "Vengeance is mine, thus says the Lord." A scripture his father taught him many years ago when discussing mercy for others and turning the other cheek even when someone does you wrong. By this time, Toby has begun to believe his partner is one of the suspects in his father's murder. Brite's treatment of civilians is unethical, appalling, and racist. One night after their shift, Toby finally accepts Brite's invitation to join him and a couple of officers for a game of pool. While enjoying his coworker's company over a few drinks and laughter, a young male walk in, approaches Officer Brite, and asks to speak with him outside.

"OK, after you," says Brite. As they proceed out the door, without warning, Brite breaks his beer bottle on the young man's head. Absolutely startled and taken back by the assault, Toby immediately acts to separate the two men and to render aid to the victim.

After the separation, Toby asks his partner, "What the hell is going on, dude? Why did you hit him from behind? I thought the two of you were going outside to talk." Toby shouts, "This man was no threat to you. There must be a report made."

Brite looks at Toby and replies, "A report is not necessary for a low-life druggie. Besides, you have no witnesses, just look around."

Toby stands face to face with his partner and repeats, "There absolutely should be a report."

"Look, Toby, I said a report is not necessary. Do I make myself clear? If you want to call EMS, be my guest, but we all know that this boy came in staggering, drunk, looking for a fight, and when he approached me in a threatening manner, I had to defend myself, so I hit him with the beer bottle. This is the story you recall as well, right, Toby?"

In total disbelief, Toby looks at his partner, then takes another look around the pub and realizes that he and the victim are the only two African Americans in the establishment. So reluctantly, Toby does not file a report and calls for medical assistance for the young man. After that night, Toby decides to meet with Mayor Brown regarding his speculation and experiences since starting on the force. A couple of days later, Toby meets the mayor and requests that their conversation remain discreet, and the mayor agrees.

"So, tell me, Toby, to what do I owe this visit? You relocated here a couple of years ago, so having you here today raises some concerns for me. Are you OK?" asks the mayor.

"All right, I am not quite sure how to say this, but as you know, I have been working in law enforcement for some time now, and from what I have witnessed, my suspicions lead me to believe that I have found one of the suspects involved in my father's murder."

The mayor looks at Toby as though he has seen a ghost and asks Toby who he believes the assailant is. Toby tells the mayor he suspects his partner, Officer Michael S. Brite, and is in the process of building a case. "Wow, Toby, now that was a gut puncher and hit very close to home. Please know that I am here in support of you and will follow your lead, so please keep me posted. What you are doing is very much commendable and is to be honored. If your father were here, he would be so proud of you. A conviction for the death of your father is long overdue. I love your father as a brother, and after his death, my wife faithfully stayed in contact with your mother to ensure you all were OK and did not have any needs. Your father was a well-known, well-respected, godly man who gave back to his community. Malcolm's credence was paying it forward and providing for those individuals that cannot provide for themselves is very much fulfilling and purposeful. Most of all, he had a soft spot for single mothers because his mother was a single mother after the passing of your granddad. Are you aware that your father was a major stakeholder in the orphanage and assisted living for single parent homes? If your grandmother were not alive, Malcolm and his siblings could have been orphans after your grandfather's death.

"Mayor, I really do appreciate all the love and support you and Mrs. Brown have shown. Since my father's demise, I have had difficulty sleeping and recalling certain events from that night, so I took it upon myself to see a therapist, and the sessions have been very beneficial. I learned that I suffer from dissociative amnesia, which means I suppress or cannot recall traumatic events. Events that are very critical in bringing the alleged murderers to justice. So the therapist advised me to revisit the most hurtful event in my life by contacting the individuals who helped me the night of my dad's beating."

"Are you going to do it?" the mayor asks.

"Yes, sir, I must revisit the past in order to move on and close this chapter of my life. 'I must allow myself to live and enjoy all that life has to offer' is what my father would always say. All I do is live and be the best me I can be."

"It sounds like you are headed in the right direction, Toby. Just remember, I am a phone call away."

"All right, Mayor, stay safe, and I will keep you posted." After extensive searching, Toby locates the phone number of the couple that helped him and his father that fatal night. Toby learns that the couple moved to South Dakota three years prior. Full of anxiety and fear, Toby gives the Willhursts a call, not knowing what to expect.

In a calm, pleasant voice, Mr. Willhurst answers, "Hello. David Willhurst, how may I help you?"

With hesitation and fear, Toby responds, "Hello, Mr. Willhurst, my name is Toby Freeman. You may not remember me, but you and your wife—"

Immediately David interrupts Toby and says, "How could we ever forget you? This is a pleasant surprise. I have been awaiting your call for some time now. How are you?"

"I am doing as well as can be expected. I am now a police officer and am investigating my father's murder. Which is why I am reaching out to you and Mrs. Willhurst."

"Unfortunately, the misses passed away two years ago, but we always wondered what became of you."

"Mr. Willhurst, I am terribly sorry to hear of your loss."

"Thank you. I appreciate your condolences. I cannot go a day without thinking about her; however, I am grateful we were able to move closer to family in her final stages of life. Sara

loved children, and hearing sounds of laughter and little patter-
ing feet from our grandchildren brought her much joy. Enough
about us. How can I be of help to you, Toby?"

"Yes, sir, Mr. Willhurst, I have a few questions regarding
that dreadful night, so I would appreciate any assistance you
can provide."

"No problem."

After hours of conversating, David helps Toby recount some
vital information he had suppressed, so before hanging up,
Toby asks one last question. "Do you recall your conversation
or your attempts to converse with my dad before being tak-
en away?" "Let me see, I cannot say there is anything more to
share. I think we pretty much covered everything. No, wait!
There is something your father said, now that I think of it. He
said, 'cops and finger.'"

"Say what?" Toby asks.

"Yes, I remember now. Your father said 'cops and finger' in
his faint voice. I was not sure if he mentioned finger because his
hands were damaged and hurting from the repeated blows of
the nightstick. I am not sure, Toby, but it may be something you
want to review in his autopsy report. Were his fingers or hands
broken, from what you recall?"

In a state of pain and anger, Toby responds, "No, there were
no broken bones in my father's hands indicated in the autopsy,
but my intuition tells me what finger he was referring to."

"You do?"

"Yes, sir. If ever I needed you to serve as a witness and testify in court regarding your role in assisting my father that night, would you be willing to do so?"

"Toby, you never have to ask me twice. I just need to know the time and place."

"Mr. Willhurst, I will be in touch." While battling mixed emotions, Toby keeps his composure and continues working with his partner as required. With the finger still ringing true in his mind, he asks his partner about his finger. "You know Mike, I must say, as long as we have been partners, I have never seen your hands without gloves."

"Excuse me! My gloves!"

"Yes, I was wondering why you never work without gloves."

Brite responds in an offhanded way and says fingerprints cannot be traced if gloves are worn. In a gust of laughter, Brite says in all sincerity that he is self-conscious of his hands because he lost his index finger over twenty years ago while trying to apprehend a prisoner, and his fingers can be a distraction. Still bothered and unable to forget the assault that took place involving his partner at the pub, Toby reaches out to Evan Pounce, the young man involved. He expects Evan to be evasive and a bit hesitant about meeting, but oddly enough Evan is very much thrilled and eager to meet up. During their meeting, Toby learns that Evan is the biological—or would you say disowned son of Officer Brite. "Hold on, I need you to explain why your father would threaten your life that night." Evan explains that he had been conversing with his father regarding some answers he needs regarding closure for him and his mother. "What closure are you looking for?" asks Toby.

"OK, listen," says Evan. "My mother was a prostitute for more than twenty years, and I am not ashamed to say it, because to me, she was the best mother a child could ask for. She did the best she could to raise a son, her secret lover's child. A child he would never acknowledge and claim because he feared losing his wife and children."

"So, you are telling me that your mother dealt with Brite knowing he had a wife and children?"

"Yes, but it was more by force than choice. He really was her pimp, because he would take the little money she had and distribute what he wanted her to have, and sadly enough, she accepted that treatment and eventually fell in love with a man who never loved or respected her or their son. That night at the pub, I tracked his location, and I was going to expose him for being the worthless lowlife he is, and he knew it, because weeks prior he texted me and told me that he was sorry to hear of my mother's death and he would give me some money to help me until I found a job. Currently I am living in a shelter because I lost everything once my mom died, and as you can see, he is a liar and manipulator. His attack on me was his way of shutting me up and deflecting what I was about to expose."

"Have you spoken to him since your assault?" asks Toby.

"Yes, he reached out and told me if I ever try a stunt like that again or ever contact his wife and children, he will make sure I pay my mother a permanent visit."

"Wait…wait, he really said that to you?"

"Yes, he said it in a voice mail."

"Do you still have that message?"

"Of course," Evan replies. "I need this for evidence if ever I went missing or died. Officer Toby, that man is dangerous, and he would kill me if he could. Why do you think I met him in a public setting? But I still underestimated him, not thinking he would lay me out for all to see, but he did. Years ago, when my mother informed him of her pregnancy, he tried to kill her, and the only reason he was unsuccessful is because she got to her gun in time and shot his finger off."

"So that is how he lost his finger?" asks Toby.

"Yes, sir. Why? Did he tell you something different?"

"Your father told me that he lost his finger while trying to apprehend an inmate." Toby looks at Evan and gives him some money and some resources in town that can help him until he finds a job. "Evan, please take care of yourself and stay away from your dad. I believe his time is soon to come. All the wrongs and injustices he has committed through the years will come to pass, and he will be in the judgment seat, for sure."

Evan tells Toby before leaving to watch and protect himself as well. "You really do not know my dad and the extremes he will go to protect himself. I am not sure how true it is, but I heard his previous partner did not die at the hands of civilian, but at the hands of my father."

Toby turns back around and says, "Do you want to run that by me again?"

"Yes, I was told that my dad paid a civilian to take his partner out because his partner found out about a few murders he and another officer committed."

"Who was the other officer your dad's partner was speaking about?" asks Toby.

Evan says, "His friend and coworker, Officer Landen."

Toby's eyes get bigger than a fifty-cent piece. When Toby hears the name Landen, a cold chill shoot through his body. There is no way Toby can hold onto such incriminating information without informing his and Brite's superior, the chief of police, Markus Bell.

Toby goes to the chief of police, Markus Bell, to voice his concerns about all he had witnessed and heard while on duty with Officer Brite throughout the partnership. With a startling look upon his face and his eyebrows raised, Chief Bell asks Toby to repeat himself, and immediately the Chief tells Toby to never mention or speak of those occurrences.

"Excuse me, Chief, did you just tell me to basically forget and write off what I know and have been told, sir?"

"That is correct, Toby. I have only a few months left in the force, and I do not want my career stained by speculations."

Toby in the most respectful manner tells the chief that at that moment all his respect for him has gone down the drain. "I am telling you that you have not one but a couple of crooked officers on the force, and your concern is your image and not the lives of those taken and destroyed by officers who choose not to honor the code of ethics and what they were sworn by. Is that what you are saying to me? At this point, Chief, you can say what you want and do what you want to do but hear me and hear me good. The officers involved, and this precinct, will be exposed. Do I make myself clear? I do not know about you, but what I can say about me is that I came onto the force with one goal and one goal only. However, through perseverance, my father and God, I have been shielded and protected for such as a time as this. I will lay my life and badge on the line to bring down whoever challenges me and my ethics."

As Toby proceeds out the door, the chief falls back in his chair and asks Toby for forgiveness. "I am wrong, and I admit my wrong, Officer Toby. I am aware of your family's tragedy and the hurt his demise caused when no one was brought to justice. However, in this small town, many people are controlled by politics and monetary influence. I am wrong, and you are right: what happened to your father and many other families in this city should never have happened. I have great respect for you, Officer Toby. Your parents raised an exceptional young man with honorable principles and morals. You can count on me. I will work with you to bring these officers to justice. Fear and denial have kept me bound for many years. I was instructed by some politicians and other elite influencers to never touch Officer Michael S. Brite due to his affiliation with key players in the city." Shortly after Toby's meeting with the chief of police, they work together to get an arrest warrant for both officers, Brite and Landen. As expected, in interrogation, both officers turned on the other. The officer's bond, oath, integrity, and agreement shifted. In efforts to protect themselves, both agreed to testify against the other in court for a lesser sentence. While out on bond and awaiting court, Officer Brite could have never imagined the devastation and loss he would endure prior to his court appearance. His wife of many years, Diane Brite served him with divorce papers. Diane expressed the deep hurt, embarrassment, and pain she has carried for many years. She tells her husband that her entire marriage and life with him has been a lie. I should have and could have divorced you a long time ago, but I did not because I loved you and with that love, I forsake myself and my feelings for yours. Not wanting to ruin your image and reputation, when all the while, you had no commitment to me or our children. No more Michael, I am doing what should have been done a long time ago. I have known for years about your son Evan. Yes, little Evan whom you conceived with your longtime girlfriend and prostitute. I have not and would not ever hold anything against your son because he had no choice in the matter. How can I be angry or resentful of our children's brother? After all, he nor our children cannot help their father is a Low Life Scum that takes advantage of women. So, tell me Michael, how long were you going to keep your son a secret, Diane asks? With complete shock and defeat on his face, Officer Brite falls to his knees begging Diane to stay with him. He expresses how much he needs her now, more than ever. I cannot get through this alone Diane. Exactly Michael! It has always been about you, never me or your children. All this time, I mustard a smile, saving face to protect what I thought was a marriage and family for the sake of you. While being tormented and crying in silence on the inside. Where did we go wrong, Michael? Wait! No need to answer, it is much too late for that now. I pray for your soul and hope you find remorse for the many lives you destroyed, you selfish jerk. Before walking away, Diane kisses Michael on the forehead and pats his back, while whispering in his ear, "Your day of judgement is soon to come, and may the lord have mercy on your soul". In a moment of vulnerability, Michael shouts! Baby please let me explain? No Michael! You have had many years to explain but chose not to, so I chose not to stay in a marriage that never was.

How could you father a child outside of our union? I would have never done that to you. You sicken me, Diane says. Soon enough you will have more than enough time to sit and think about your actions and the brokenness it causes our family and so many others.

After two long years of court appeals, both officers meet their fate with the help of two key witnesses from the pub assault, Mr. Willhurst, Evan Pounce's DNA, and voice recordings along with a surprising testimony from none other than Officer Toby Freeman. A disgrace to the force, Toby states while on the stand. Recounts from all the witnesses aid in proving how malicious, vile, and malevolent the two officers really are. Officer Michael S. Brite is found guilty and sentenced to life without parole for two counts of second-degree murder, assault, drug trafficking, prostitution and organized crime. Further evidence proves that Officer Landen in fact murder Officer Brite's former partner, and Landen is sentenced to forty-five years to life for first-degree murder, accessory to murder, and prostitution by the courts. After the verdict is read, Toby says to his father, with tears in his eyes, "Dad, I hope you are proud of me, because I am proud of you and Mom for raising me to be the man I am today: passionate, determined, and a man of God. Go on and rest now, and do not worry about me and Mom; we are just fine. I will see you again one day, and we can finish our one-on-one game of bless ball."

After sentencing, Toby stayed with the force for fifteen more years, and during that time, Toby was personally nominated by the chief of police to assume his role after he retired. Toby was selected and accepted the position with great humility. Their relationship grew stronger once Chief Bell retired, and they served as a great support system for each other through the years. As a tribute to his father and other citizens in the city who had been victimized by officers of the law, Toby developed a foundation, the Foundation of Hope, Honor, and Justice, for all people. He implemented standards and regulations to abide by, along with a task force of officers sworn to bring down and expose the unlawful officers. His purpose-driven desire was to leave a mark and a team of officers striving for the same humanitarian goals to live by and providing fair and just treatment to all citizens.

Printed in the USA
CPSIA information can be obtained
at www.ICGtesting.com
LVHW020736220324
775103LV00012B/82